TURKEY TROUBLE ON THE NATIONAL MALL

by **Ron Roy**
illustrated by **Timothy Bush**

A STEPPING STONE BOOK™
Random House 🏠 New York

Dedicated to readers all:
big and small, short and tall
—R.R.

Photo credits: pp. 90–91, courtesy of the Library of Congress.

Text copyright © 2012 by Ron Roy
Interior illustrations copyright © 2012 by Timothy Bush
Cover art copyright © 2012 by Greg Swearingen

Visit us on the Web!
SteppingStonesBooks.com
randomhouse.com/kids

Educators and librarians, for a variety of teaching tools, visit us at RHTeachersLibrarians.com

Library of Congress Cataloging-in-Publication Data
Roy, Ron.
Turkey trouble on the National Mall / by Ron Roy ; illustrated by Timothy Bush.
 p. cm. — (Capital mysteries ; #14)
"A Stepping Stone book."
Summary: "KC and Marshall convince the President of the United States to pardon more than one turkey for Thanksgiving, but all 117 of them are stolen off the National Mall."—Provided by publisher.
ISBN 978-0-307-93220-4 (pbk.) — ISBN 978-0-375-87004-0 (lib. bdg.) — ISBN 978-0-307-97575-1 (ebook)
[1. Mystery and detective stories—Fiction. 2. Turkeys—Fiction.
3. Presidents—Family—Fiction. 4. Stealing—Fiction. 5. Thanksgiving Day—Fiction. 6. Washington (D.C.)—Fiction.] I. Title.
PZ7.R8139Tur 2012 [Fic]—dc23 2011051794

Printed in the United States of America
10 9 8 7 6 5

Contents

1
Turkey Talk

"I didn't know turkey feathers were so smooth," Marshall said. Next to him stood a large white turkey with a black circle around one eye. Marshall ran his fingers along the turkey's broad back.

KC tossed some popcorn on the ground. She and Marshall watched the turkey dip his head and gobble up the food. It was early Monday morning, three days before Thanksgiving, and they were on the White House lawn. KC had lived in the White House since her mother married the President of the United States.

"I'm glad the president is pardoning this turkey," KC said. Every Thanksgiving, the President of the United States gave one turkey a pardon. That meant the turkey wouldn't be part of Thanksgiving dinner. "He's going to Mount Vernon to live."

"You mean he's going to George Washington's house?" Marshall asked.

KC nodded. "There's a big farm there now, with lots of animals."

The turkey finished eating the popcorn. He started picking at KC's sneaker laces. "Hey, Marsh, let's give him a name," KC said.

Marshall looked at the black circle around the turkey's left eye. "How about Spot?" he said.

The turkey let out a loud *gobble gobble!*

KC laughed. "He doesn't seem to think Spot is a good name," she said. "Besides, it sounds like a dog's name. Why don't we call him Cloud?"

"Because he's white?" Marshall asked.

"And because he's big and soft," KC said. She held out a handful of popcorn. "Do you like your new name?"

2

The turkey dipped his head and ate out of KC's hand.

"He likes it!" KC said.

"When does Cloud go to Mount Vernon?" Marshall asked.

"The day after Thanksgiving," KC said. "The president said we're going to drive him there. Want to come?"

"Sure," Marshall said. "Are there other turkeys for Cloud to play with?"

"I don't know," KC said. She looked at Cloud, then grinned at Marshall. "You just gave me a great idea!"

"I did?" Marshall asked. "Are you going to tell me what it is?"

KC and Marshall left Cloud's pen, and KC latched the gate behind them. "Yes, but I want to tell Mom and the president at the same time," KC said. "Race you!"

KC and Marshall bolted around the rose garden and into the White House. They charged up some stairs, around a corner, and past Arnold, the marine guard standing in front of the private quarters.

KC could hear her mom laughing in the kitchen. She and Marshall walked toward the sound.

"Hi, Mom. Hi, Yvonne," KC said.

Yvonne had come from France to work in the president's private residence. She planned meals, shopped, and cooked for the First Family. She looked after KC, too, like an aunt.

"Hi," KC's mom greeted them. She and Yvonne were sitting at the kitchen table sharing sections of the newspaper.

"Only a half hour before school," Yvonne said. "Would you like some cereal?"

"Yes please." KC pulled out a chair. "Can I talk to the president?" she asked her mother. "I have a great idea for Thanksgiving!"

Yvonne set a bowl of cereal in front of

KC. She handed Marshall a glass of juice.

Her mother grinned. "Now you've got me curious," she said. "How about a hint?"

"She won't even tell me!" Marshall said.

"Won't tell you what?" a voice said from behind Marshall.

The president walked into the kitchen. He was tall, and his dark hair had a little gray around his ears. With him was Vice President Mary Kincaid.

"I have an idea, Dad," KC told him. "It's about Congress."

The president sat next to his wife. "You're too young to run for Congress," he said to his stepdaughter.

KC giggled. "You know the turkey you're going to pardon?" she asked him.

"Big fellow with white feathers?" he said. "We're taking him to Mount Vernon on Friday."

"We named him Cloud," Marshall said.

"Nice name," the president said. "So what's your idea?"

"Well, Cloud might be lonely on the farm. He should have playmates," KC said. "So I was thinking, we could pardon—I mean *you* could pardon—a bunch of other turkeys to go to Mount Vernon with him!"

"Other turkeys?" the president echoed.

KC grinned. "You could ask all the senators to pardon their turkeys," she said. "You could ask all the members of the House of Representatives to pardon their turkeys, too. Then the turkeys could go to live at Mount Vernon together!"

"Goodness!" Yvonne said, setting mugs of coffee in front of the president and vice president. "That would be hundreds of turkeys!"

"Five hundred and thirty-six, to be exact," the vice president said.

Marshall nearly choked on his juice.

2
Pardon Me!

"Sweetheart, I don't know," the president said. "The senators and members of the House make their own Thanksgiving plans. I can't tell them what to do and what to eat."

"I know," said KC. "But couldn't you ask?"

"And what if they agree?" KC's mom asked. "I hope you're not suggesting they bring their turkeys to the White House."

"How about there?" Marshall said. He pointed to a headline in the newspaper that said NATIONAL MALL TO GET NEW LAWN THIS SPRING. "There's tons of room!"

"We can't bring hundreds of turkeys to the National Mall," the president said. "Who would take care of them?"

"I would, and Marshall would help me," KC said.

Everyone looked at Marshall.

Marshall just shrugged.

"I like KC's idea," the vice president said. "I'll bet a lot of senators and representatives would pardon their turkeys if asked."

The president shook his head. "I don't feel it's the president's place to ask others not to eat turkey on Thanksgiving," he said. "But I'm still going to pardon Cloud!"

KC's mother gave her a hug. "Time for school," she said. "Take some fruit."

KC and Marshall each chose an apple from the bowl and headed downstairs.

"Sorry our idea—I mean your idea—got chopped," Marshall said.

"Who says it got chopped?" KC asked.

"Well, you heard what the president said," Marshall said.

KC grinned. "Maybe he can't ask people

not to eat turkey on Thanksgiving," she said. "But I sure can!"

The last class of the day was art. KC drew a huge picture of Cloud. She used the biggest drawing paper Ms. Vango, the art teacher, had. She drew a black circle around his left eye, then used a red crayon for the wattle that hung under his chin. The picture was almost life-sized.

"Great drawing," Marshall said. "It looks just like Cloud."

"Thank you." KC carefully folded the picture and placed it inside her backpack. Then she asked Ms. Vango if she could take home another large sheet of drawing paper and a black marker.

"Take two sheets," Ms. Vango said. "Are you and Marshall doing an art project at the White House?"

"Something like that!" KC said.

When the bell rang, KC and Marshall were the first kids out the door.

"What are you up to now?" Marshall asked as they headed down the street.

KC just grinned.

A short walk took them to the wide marble steps of the Capitol building. KC dropped her backpack on one of the steps. She took out her picture of Cloud, unfolded it, and handed it to Marshall. "Hold this, please," she said.

"Not until you tell me what we're doing here!" Marshall said. "This is the Capitol!"

KC pulled out one of the sheets of drawing paper and the marker.

"I know that," she said. "Congresspeople come here all day long. And they're all going to see our sign."

"What sign?"

KC sat on the step and began writing on the drawing paper. "The sign asking people to pardon their turkeys this year!" she said. "The sign I'm making right now!"

"But you can't do that!" Marshall said, plopping down next to her.

"Who says?" KC asked. "It's a free country!"

"The president says, that's who," said Marshall.

"He said *he* didn't want to ask people to pardon their turkeys this year," KC said. "But I'll do it instead!"

Marshall watched as KC made big block letters on the paper. "I have a feeling this is going to get us in trouble," he said.

"Don't worry, I'll take the blame," KC said. "And if I go to jail, you can bring me cookies."

Marshall grinned. "Okay. What's your sign going to say?" he asked.

KC finished what she was writing, then held the poster up so Marshall could read it.

THIS IS CLOUD, THE WHITE HOUSE
TURKEY. THE PRESIDENT IS GOING
TO PARDON HIM. CLOUD IS GOING
TO A FARM AT MOUNT VERNON
TO LIVE HAPPILY EVER AFTER.
WON'T YOU PLEASE PARDON YOUR
TURKEY, TOO? BRING YOUR LIVE
TURKEY TO THE PEN ON THE
NATIONAL MALL BEFORE
THANKSGIVING. THANK YOU!

"KC, there is no turkey pen on the National Mall," Marshall said.

"Not yet," KC said. "Now you hold the picture of Cloud, and I'll hold the sign."

Marshall sighed. He stood up with the picture in front of his chest. "I feel like a turkey," he muttered.

KC giggled. "You look like one, too!" she told him.

A lot of tourists read KC's sign and looked

at her drawing of Cloud. Most just smiled and kept walking.

"Cool turkey," one man said.

A jogger stopped running, read the sign, and shook his head. "No turkey on Thanksgiving? No way!" Then he kept on running.

"No one wants to give up their turkey," Marshall said after they'd been standing there for a half hour.

KC didn't say anything. She felt disappointed. She had recognized a few of the men and women who hurried past, carrying briefcases. They were senators and representatives. She'd seen them on TV and at the White House.

"There you are!" a familiar voice said from behind KC.

The vice president strode toward the kids, holding her cell phone to her ear. She dropped the phone into her briefcase. Then she read KC's sign and admired the drawing. "So you're still trying to get people to give up their turkeys?" she asked KC.

KC nodded. "But Marshall and I are the only two who think it's a good idea," she said.

"Well, count me in," the vice president said. "Once people hear about your idea, I think we'll get a lot of turkeys. And I'll try to win the president over, too. If we can convince other people, I'll ask the president to build a pen on the National Mall!"

A tall man in a dark suit stopped. "Hello, Vice President Kincaid," he said. "What brings you here?"

The vice president smiled. "Hello, Senator Scott. Have you met KC, the president's stepdaughter? KC and her friend Marshall are asking people to consider pardoning their turkeys this year. How about it, Senator Scott?"

The senator read KC's sign. "Like the president does every year, right?" he asked.

"Yes, sir," KC said. "Wouldn't it be wonderful to know that your turkey was living on a farm, playing with other turkeys?"

The senator smiled. "You're very convincing, young lady. I'll talk to Mrs. Scott tonight. But you've already sold me on the idea!"

KC and Marshall beamed. "Thank you!" they both cried.

As soon as people began to recognize the vice president, a crowd formed around KC and Marshall. The kids tried hard to convince everyone to pardon a turkey and to bring it to the pen.

By the time KC, Marshall, and the vice president left for the White House, hundreds of people had read KC's sign. Many of them thought it was a terrific idea to pardon their own turkeys.

"When can I bring my turkey to the pen?" a congresswoman asked.

"Tomorrow afternoon," the vice president said. Then she whispered to KC and Marshall, "If I can get a certain president to agree!"

Later, the president listened to Mary Kincaid and the kids as they told him about meeting people on the Capitol steps.

"Maybe you're not too young to run for Congress," he told KC. "Okay, I'm convinced. Let's get Operation Turkey moving. Mary, how fast can you get that pen built?"

3
Turkey Troubles

Overnight, carpenters built a pen on the lawn in front of the Smithsonian Castle on the National Mall.

On Tuesday, the vice president told KC and Marshall that their campaign was off to a huge start. "It's catching on!" she said. "I'm getting dozens of phone calls and e-mails. People stop me on the street. They want to pardon their turkeys this year!"

Tuesday night and early Wednesday morning, more and more live turkeys were delivered to the pen on the Mall. The vice president ordered ten sacks of turkey feed.

Two park rangers were assigned to take care of the turkeys. Both of the rangers decided they would pardon their families' turkeys, too.

People brought more turkeys on Wednesday. Tourists visiting from all over the world stopped to look at them. There was a line of cars on 14th Street. People climbed out of the cars and carried their turkeys to the pen. One man came on a bicycle with his turkey in a basket!

KC and Marshall were dismissed early from school on Wednesday, for the Thanksgiving holiday. They rushed to the White House and into the kitchen. "How many turkeys now?" KC asked her mother.

"Nearly a hundred," Lois said. "And more on the way!"

"This is great!" KC said. "Today we're bringing Cloud to the Mall, right?"

"Arnold and his brother are waiting to drive you," Yvonne said. "But go upstairs and change first."

The president had asked the marine guard Arnold and his brother, Dez, to transport Cloud to his new pen on the Mall in Dez's truck. The two men sat up front, while KC and Marshall climbed into the open bed of the truck, where Cloud waited in a small crate. A thick layer of straw on the floor made it soft and comfortable. Two sleeping bags lay on the straw.

"Why do you have sleeping bags and stuff back here?" KC asked Dez.

"Arnold and I took our little cousins on a hayride a few days ago," Dez said, laughing. "They crawled into the sleeping bags and fell asleep after about twenty minutes!"

KC fed Cloud another handful of popcorn through the wire of the crate. "Wait till you see where you're going!" she said to the turkey.

Dez's truck left the White House grounds through a rear gate. The truck bounced across the lawn at the National Mall. Dez stopped in front of the new turkey pen.

KC and Marshall ran up to the wire-and-wood pen. They had to squeeze through a lot of people lined up at the fence. The two park rangers were inside the pen, which was filled with noisy turkeys. It was like an ocean of moving feathers. Kids were yelling questions at the park rangers.

"Why are most of the turkeys white?"

"What do they eat?"

"How do you tell boy turkeys from girl turkeys?"

Arnold and Dez took Cloud out of the crate and carried him over to the pen.

"Wait, I have a present for him," KC said. She pulled a silver bell on a string from her pocket. She tied the bell around Cloud's neck.

"What's that for?" Marshall asked.

"It'll be easier to find him when we visit him at Mount Vernon," KC said. "We'll be able to hear the bell!"

Arnold put Cloud into the pen and closed the gate. Right away, the forty-pound white turkey marched over to the other turkeys. He was taller than most of them, so KC and Marshall could follow him as he strutted about. The bell jingled as he walked.

KC and Marshall watched the rangers spread straw inside the pen and fill trays with food pellets and fresh water.

One of the rangers stopped, looked over KC's head, and said, "Uh-oh, here comes trouble."

KC and Marshall turned around. Marching across the National Mall lawn were six men and women. Each one wore a bright red T-shirt with EET written across the front. Below the initials were the words EAT EVERY TURKEY.

A few of the marchers carried signs. The signs said TURKEYS ARE FOOD, NOT PETS.

A man with black hair in a ponytail walked over to KC and Marshall. "I'm Barney Gibble," he said. "I see your little campaign is off to a good start. How many more turkeys are you expecting?"

"We don't know," KC said. "A thousand, I hope!"

"This is ridiculous," Barney Gibble said. "People should be eating turkeys, not making pets out of them."

"We're not saying they can't," Marshall said. "Anyone can have turkey on Thanksgiving if they want to!"

"People do have a choice," Barney Gibble said. He had raised his voice, and some of the people around him started listening. "In fact, we're serving turkey tomorrow night to anyone who wants a real Thanksgiving meal! Eight o'clock at Twelve New Street."

"Visitors, Boss," one of the women holding a sign mumbled to Barney Gibble.

A bright blue van crossed the lawn. From the top sprouted a TV satellite dish. White letters on the side of the van said DONNY DRUM NEWS HOUR! with Donny Drum's smiling face under the words.

KC recognized Donny Drum when he leaped out of the van. He was the news anchor for a TV show that aired five evenings a week. The man had blond hair, big white teeth, and sly-looking blue eyes.

"Donny Drum," the news anchor said as he strode toward the kids, rangers, and turkeys. He held a microphone. A man with a camera walked behind him. "Hello, Ms. Corcoran. I see you're making news for the White House! Care to tell my viewers about your 'Save the Turkey' campaign?"

"She's not making news," Barney Gibble said. "She's just trying to tell the American people what they can and can't eat for Thanksgiving! She's being a little pest!"

"PEST, PEST, PEST!" the T-shirt-wearing people shouted behind Barney Gibble, who took a step forward.

"Okay, back off!" one of the rangers warned.

"Who are you telling to back off?" Barney Gibble asked, puffing out his chest.

Donny Drum's white teeth, microphone, and camera swung around to Barney Gibble. "And you are . . . ?" Donny Drum asked, pointing his microphone at Barney's chin.

KC grabbed Marshall's arm to pull him away. "Come on, let's get out of here."

"But it was just getting good!" Marshall said.

As KC and Marshall backed away from the crowd, KC noticed a long green truck parked on the edge of the lawn. *That's probably the truck to take the turkeys to Mount Vernon,* KC thought. She hoped the long drive wouldn't scare Cloud and his friends.

After supper, the president, Lois, and KC watched the Donny Drum news show. The news anchor's face appeared, his white teeth gleaming. "Good evening, friends! Donny Drum here, and I have news for you!"

Then his face faded, and the next thing viewers saw was the top of the Smithsonian Castle on the National Mall. The camera panned down until it showed the pen filled with turkeys.

"Wow!" the president said. "It looks like your idea has caught on, KC."

KC swallowed. Before she could say anything, her own face came onto the TV. She was standing next to Marshall with people and turkeys behind them.

"KC, that's you!" her mother cried out. "When—"

"Shhh," the president said. "Let's listen."

They saw and heard the ranger tell Barney Gibble to back off, and then the camera landed on Barney's face. "We need to feed people," he said into the camera, "not treat turkeys as family pets!"

The camera came back to Donny Drum, who was grinning. "And I assume you'll be sitting down to a turkey dinner yourself tomorrow, Mr. Gibble?"

Barney Gibble's face filled the screen. "You bet I will!" he said. "My EET friends and I are hosting a huge turkey dinner at eight o'clock tomorrow night. Everyone is welcome, ten bucks a person. The address is Twelve New Street. Come eat with EET!"

The president clicked off the TV. "Care to walk over to the Mall and show me these turkeys?" he asked KC. "Natasha needs some exercise, too." Natasha was the president's pet greyhound.

A few minutes later, KC clipped the leash on to the greyhound's collar as the First Family headed away from the White House

grounds. It was dark and quiet on Pennsylvania Avenue. A cool wind blew through
the bare tree branches, making a whistling
sound.

Four secret service agents walked silently
with them, two in front and two in back.
They were all dressed in black and had
earbuds in their ears. KC walked between
her mom and President Thornton, holding
Natasha's leash.

KC laughed. "Wait till you hear how noisy
the turkeys are!" she said. "I'm surprised we
can't hear them from the White House!"

But as the group crossed the National
Mall's wide lawn, not a sound could be
heard. And as they approached the turkey
pen, KC saw why. The turkeys, every single
one, were gone.

4
Crafty Eyes

"It's EET," KC said the next morning. "Who else would steal one hundred seventeen turkeys the day before Thanksgiving?"

KC and Marshall were in KC's room. The night before, the president had called the director of the FBI about the theft. Detectives had gone to the Mall to look for evidence. All they found were feathers and hundreds of muddy footprints. The detectives couldn't tell if the footprints were left by tourists or by the thieves.

The FBI director had promised that his team would do their best to track down the stolen turkeys.

Marshall gulped. "Do you think EET plans to eat the turkeys tonight at the big dinner?" he asked.

"I don't know." KC pulled a newspaper off a pile she kept neatly stacked on a shelf.

Marshall moved KC's stuffed animals so he could sit on the bed. "Hey, Mr. Giraffe has only one eye," he said.

"I know," KC said, spreading the newspaper on her bed. She neatly arranged each section of the newspaper. Local News, World News, Sports, Fashion, Travel and Leisure, Comics.

In the local section, she looked for anything about EET. She found it quickly.

KC sat up, holding the paper in her lap. "Look at this ad, Marsh," she said.

Come and gobble turkey! Enjoy a traditional turkey dinner at 8:00 p.m. on Thanksgiving. All the turkey and fixings you can eat for ten dollars per person. Bring your appetite! 12 New Street.

"We have to stop him," KC said. "If he stole Cloud and all those other turkeys, he should go to jail!" She threw the paper on the floor and jumped off her bed.

"But we don't know he did it," Marshall reminded her.

KC ran into her bathroom. Marshall could hear her brushing her teeth. He quickly reread the ad about EET's dinner. Then he noticed a story in the World News section.

KC came out of the bathroom and grabbed her favorite boots.

"Someone else is having turkey troubles," Marshall said. He showed the story to KC. The headline read AVIAN FLU WIPES OUT BIRDS IN EUROPE. A picture showed dead birds on the ground.

KC leaned in to read the article.

Scientists are concerned. "Birds are dying," says Dr. Louis Alvarez. "Poultry farmers are losing business as chickens and turkeys perish. In Paris, millinery shops are closing because they can no longer find enough turkey feathers to make their hats. Marie Le Roi, owner of the shop Les Chapeaux, says, "I rely on turkey feathers for most of my hats. But for the past few weeks, I cannot buy new feathers. My customers are very upset!"

"That's awful," KC said with a determined look on her face. She sat on the floor and pulled on her boots.

"Are we going somewhere?" Marshall asked.

"You bet we are!" KC said. "We're going to Twelve New Street to see Mr. Barney Bibble!"

"I think it's Gibble," Marshall said.

"Whatever. We're going!" KC answered.

She and Marshall pulled on warm sweaters, grabbed a couple of apples, and left the White House.

Near the Treasury Department building, a skateboarder zoomed up and stopped next to KC and Marshall. It was a teenager with freckles.

"Dudes, you like pizza?" he asked, thrusting two red flyers into their hands.

"Yeah, why?" KC asked.

"Read it," the kid said, aiming himself toward a group of tourists farther down 15th Street.

KC and Marshall looked at the papers they'd been given.

THANKSGIVING WEEK SPECIAL—
OUR OWN TURKEY PIZZA!
SERVED AT CREATIVE PIZZA,
ACROSS FROM THE
OLD POST OFFICE.

Under the words, there was a drawing of a Pilgrim eating a slice of pizza.

"Whoever heard of turkey on pizza?" KC said. She dropped her flyer into a trash can.

"Do we even know where New Street is?" Marshall asked.

"Sort of," KC said. "Yvonne told me it's up New York Avenue, on the right-hand side."

New Street turned out to be a narrow street filled with small stores and restaurants. Only a few were open on Thanksgiving morning.

"Wait, KC," Marshall said. He stopped in front of a shop window. Inside were toys, model kits, Native American stuff, craft feathers, dolls, and millions of beads. One of the displays showed glass eyes for dolls and stuffed animals. A sign hung on the door.

CRAFTY GUY CRAFTS
SPECIAL THANKSGIVING HOURS
AIDAN LEROY, PROPRIETOR

"Look at those cool Native American moccasins," Marshall said. "They sell kits!"

"Marsh, let's come back another time," KC said. "We have to find Barney Gobble."

"Gibble. Let's go in for one minute," Marshall said. "Maybe you can find an eye for your giraffe. He'll be happier with two eyes!" He took KC's hand and tugged her into the shop.

A bell jingled as the kids entered. No one seemed to be in the shop. Then they heard a swishing and clicking sound. A man stepped through strings of beads that hung in front of a small passageway. The man had black hair and shiny teeth. "May I be of service?" he asked. The man's accent reminded KC of how Yvonne spoke.

"My friend needs an eye for her giraffe," Marshall said.

"We have eyes!" the man said. "If you will follow?"

He marched down an aisle and stopped near a sort of office space. There was a phone and a laptop. He pointed to a display case. Inside were hundreds of eyes.

KC gasped. There were tiny eyes, huge eyes, glass eyes, wooden eyes. Some were black. Others were blue. Some were green. A few were red with yellow centers.

"Now, for your giraffe," the man said. "Can you pick one that matches the other eye?"

KC examined the case filled with eyes. They all seemed to be staring at her. Then she shook her head. "The eye wasn't round," she said. "More long, like . . . wait, I can draw it. Do you have a piece of paper?"

"Certainly," the man said. He grabbed a sheet of paper and handed it to KC.

KC pulled a marker from her pocket. She drew her stuffed giraffe's head and his one eye. "Like this," she said.

The man looked at the drawing. "Hmmm, difficult, I am afraid. Can you bring the giraffe in?" he asked. "It's much easier to make a good match if I see him, face to face."

"Sure," KC said. "I'll bring Mr. Giraffe in tomorrow."

"Beautiful!" the man said, flashing his brilliant teeth. *"A bientôt."*

As they were leaving, KC stopped. "Can you tell us where Twelve New Street is?" she asked.

"But of course," the man said. He pointed farther up the street. "Are you sure you want to go in there? Number Twelve is a pool hall."

5
Turkey Pizza

KC and Marshall thanked Mr. Leroy and hurried up New Street.

"A pool hall?" KC repeated. "What's a pool hall?"

"I think it's a place where people play pool," Marshall said. KC raised one eyebrow. "You know, that game where you hit colored balls with a stick into different pockets. My uncle has a pool table in his basement." He frowned. "It's a weird place to have dinner."

"I don't care. If they stole our turkeys, I'll get the president to arrest them!" KC said.

"But, KC, the dinner is tonight, in about nine hours," Marshall said.

"That's why we have to hurry!"

Four minutes later, KC and Marshall pressed their faces against the glass of a wide storefront window at 12 New Street.

There were no people inside, and the lights were off. They saw ten long tables covered with white cloths. In the middle of each table stood a vase of flowers. A big clock on one wall said 11:15.

KC wasn't looking forward to seeing Barney Gibble again, but she knew she had no choice. She walked to the door and tugged on the handle. "It's locked," she said.

Marshall pointed to a small sign taped to the window. BACK SOON. BARNEY.

"Now what?" he asked.

KC rattled the knob, but the door still wouldn't open. "We need to save Cloud!"

Marshall put a hand on KC's arm. "Um, we don't know the EET people stole the turkeys," he said. "Think about it. It would be stupid to go on TV, telling everyone they're having this turkey dinner, then steal the turkeys. Everyone would know it was EET!"

KC looked at Marshall. "You don't think it was Barney Gibble, do you?" she asked.

"I'm not sure," he said, pulling the red flyer out of his pocket. "But what about these guys?"

"What guys?"

"Creative Pizza," Marshall said, showing her the flyer. "They're serving turkey pizza. It says so right here!"

KC grabbed the flyer. Her eyes flew over the words. "You're right!" she said. "What are we waiting for?"

Marshall took the flyer back from KC. "Across from the Old Post Office," he read. "Where's that?"

"Not far," KC said. "It's between here and the National Mall. Come on!"

KC and Marshall ran down 12th Street, off New York Avenue. They were puffing for breath when they reached Pennsylvania Avenue. "There it is!" KC said.

The clock tower rose above the nearby buildings. Part of the Old Post Office's roof was made of glass, making it hard to look at when the sun's reflection bounced off.

"So where's Creative Pizza?" Marshall asked.

KC turned so the Old Post Office was behind her. "There," she said, pointing to a brick building with a red awning.

"Do we have a plan?" Marshall asked.

KC grinned. "Yes," she said. She took out her marker and the picture she'd drawn of her giraffe. Flipping the picture over, she saw some typing on the back.

She folded the paper so that she had a clean space for writing. "Let's go see the pizza guys!"

The kids headed for the awning that shaded the door to Creative Pizza.

When they walked in, a voice called out, "Welcome to Creative Pizza!"

KC and Marshall looked into the tired face of a man wearing a red apron. Behind him was an open brick oven. Two or three pizzas were cooking in the oven, sending amazing smells into the tiny restaurant.

KC walked up to the man. "I'm doing research on turkeys," she said, showing her paper and pen. It wasn't exactly a lie. "Since it's Thanksgiving and you're serving turkey pizza, can I ask you a few questions?"

"What kind of questions?" the man asked. "My boss isn't here right now."

"That's okay," KC said in her best reporter's voice. She pretended to read from her paper. "Where do you get your turkeys?"

"Where do we get 'em?" the man asked. "Beats me. But last night we got a bunch. Our turkey-pizza special goes on all next week, so we need plenty."

"You got a bunch?" Marshall asked. "And you don't know where they came from?"

The man shook his head. "I just work here, man. All I know is the turkeys came in late, and we all had to work extra hours getting them ready," he said. "I didn't get home till three this morning!"

KC gulped. "Were they white turkeys?" she asked.

"Yeah, most of 'em were white, but there were a few dark ones," the man said. "I asked my boss, and she said most turkeys we eat are white. More meat on 'em, I guess."

"Did one of them have a bell tied around its neck?" KC asked.

"No bells, no whistles, nothing but noisy turkeys and millions of feathers," the man said.

KC grabbed Marshall's arm. "Come on," she said, shoving the paper in her pocket.

"Did you hear that?" KC said after they left the restaurant. "They got turkeys late last night! Ours were stolen last night!"

"But that doesn't mean they're the same turkeys," Marshall said. He looked KC in the eye. "Please don't tell me you're going to ask the FBI to send the SWAT team to raid this pizza shop!"

KC folded her arms. "Not yet," she said. "But they are still suspects!" She heard bonging from the bell tower. "Right now, we're going to talk to Barney Nibble."

"Um, it's Gibble," Marshall said.

It was only a few minutes before KC and Marshall walked into Barney's pool hall. They heard a buzzer, then a loud voice yelling, "I'm in the kitchen!"

They followed the voice past the pool tables. A man stood with his back to them. His hands were in a deep sink, where the water was running. He had an apron around his waist, and his hair tied back in a ponytail.

Barney Gibble turned around. "It's about time," he said, then recognized KC and

Marshall from the day before. "Well, well, well. You're a little early for turkey dinner, Ms. Corcoran."

"We didn't come to eat," KC said. Her voice was shaking.

Barney Gibble wiped his hands on his apron. "Then why are you here?" he asked. "And please don't tell me I shouldn't be eating turkey for Thanksgiving."

KC took a breath, then started talking. "All the turkeys were stolen last night," she said.

"What turkeys? Wait, *your* turkeys?" Barney Gibble asked. "The ones on the National Mall?"

KC nodded.

Barney Gibble's eyebrows went up. "And you think EET stole them, right?" He crooked a finger at the kids. "Come with me. I want to show you something."

Barney led the kids into a small office

around the corner from the kitchen. The room was cramped, with a desk and chair, filing cabinets, and a cork bulletin board. Barney put a finger on a photograph pinned to the cork. "See this?" he asked. "It's my turkey farm in Vermont. I own five thousand turkeys. Why would I steal yours?"

KC and Marshall looked at the photo. It showed a lot of buildings and several thousand turkeys.

"I thought most turkeys were white," KC said. "Yours are all dark-colored."

"The white ones have more meat, but the dark ones have better flavor," Barney Gibble said. He grinned devilishly. "Which is why I'm serving them tonight. I go for flavor."

KC didn't know what else to say. But at least now she knew why Barney Gibble wanted everyone to eat turkeys—he sold them! She and Marshall followed the man through the kitchen toward the front door.

KC saw something interesting on the floor. She quickly picked up the object and shoved it in her pocket.

"Sorry we disturbed you," KC said as Barney opened the door to New Street.

"No problem," he said. "Come back tonight for dinner!"

The kids walked down New Street, then turned left when they reached New York Avenue. They could see the White House straight ahead.

"Do you believe him?" Marshall asked.

"Not in a million years," KC said, reaching into her pocket. She pulled out a white feather and showed it to Marshall. "I found this on his kitchen floor."

Marshall looked at the white feather. "What does it mean?" he asked.

"It means he's lying," KC said.

6
A French Lesson

"Lying?" Marshall said.

"Yeah, lying," KC said. "He told us he's serving turkeys with dark feathers. So what's a white feather doing on his floor?"

Marshall stroked the white feather. "This could be from a seagull," he said. "There are a lot around here."

"Right, or it could have fallen from an angel's wing!" KC said. "This is a turkey feather, Marsh. It feels and looks exactly like Cloud's feathers!"

"You're right, it does," Marshall said.

They started walking toward the White House again.

Marshall bumped KC's shoulder with his own. "You know, I don't think the thieves are going to eat the turkeys," he said.

"Why not?" KC asked.

"Well, they stole the turkey food, too," Marshall answered. "That must mean they are planning to feed the turkeys, right?"

"I hope you're right," KC said. "But where are they?"

"The crooks would need a truck," said Marshall.

"I saw one yesterday on the Mall," KC said. "But it was gone last night when we walked the dog. Gone just like the turkeys."

At the White House, Yvonne was in the kitchen. She had a couple of cookbooks open on the table. "I heard about the turkeys," Yvonne said when KC and Marshall came in. "Have you been out looking for them?"

"We tried," KC said.

"Well, the president spoke to the FBI director this morning, but I don't know if they are having any luck, either," Yvonne said. "Did you have lunch?"

"We had apples," KC said. "We're going upstairs, okay?"

"Sure. Dinner is at five o'clock," Yvonne said. "A *bientôt*."

"Ah what?" Marshall asked.

"Ah-bee-en-toe," Yvonne said, pronouncing each syllable. "It means *see you later* in French." She spelled it for the kids.

Marshall grinned at Yvonne. "Ah-bee-en-toe to you, too!" he said.

In her room, KC sat on the edge of her bed and grabbed her stuffed giraffe. "Where would you hide a hundred turkeys?" she asked Marshall.

"I don't know," Marshall said. "If the crooks had a truck, they might take them out to a farm or someplace. Put them in a barn, maybe."

"Yeah. I would, too, I guess," KC said. "There are a lot of farms around here, outside the city."

She looked at her giraffe, then fished a paper from her back pocket. It was the drawing she'd made of Mr. Giraffe's head in the Crafty Guy store. She held the picture up next to the stuffed animal.

"Hey," Marshall said. "What's that on the back of your drawing?"

KC flipped the paper over. "It's an e-mail," she said.

Marvelous, *mon frère*. I will take them all. Will e-mail again Friday. *A bientôt. Votre soeur,* MLR.

"Ah-bee-en-toe," KC read from the paper. "*He* said it, too."

"What are you talking about?" Marshall asked. "Who said it?"

KC handed Marshall the paper. "The man in the craft shop gave me this to draw on," she said. "When we left, he said what

54

Yvonne says. 'A *bientôt.*' Maybe he's French, too."

"Who's the e-mail from?" Marshall asked.

Above the word *marvelous*, KC saw a name and an e-mail address. "Someone named Marie Le Roi," she said. "In Paris, France."

KC stared over Marshall's shoulder at the wall. Her eyes didn't blink. Then she closed them.

"KC? Are you there?" Marshall asked.

Suddenly KC jumped off the bed and ran to her stack of newspapers. She found the World News section from the day before. "Here it is!" KC skimmed the article, then read part of it out loud.

"In Paris, millinery shops are closing because they can no longer find enough turkey feathers to make their hats. Marie Le Roi, owner of the shop Les Chapeaux, says, 'I rely on turkey feathers for most of my hats. But for the past few weeks, I cannot buy new feathers. My customers are very upset!'"

"I know," Marshall said. "I showed that to you yesterday. What—"

"Marsh, that hat lady in Paris sent this e-mail to the guy who owns the craft store you dragged me into! She's MLR—Marie Le Roi!" KC cried. "Don't you get it?"

Marshall just stared at her. Then his mouth fell open. "She needs turkey feathers!" he cried.

7
"This Isn't TV, Marshall"

The kids ran into the kitchen. Yvonne was sitting at the table, and KC dropped the sheet of paper in front of her.

"What's this?" Yvonne asked.

"It's an e-mail," KC said. "We think it's from a lady in France." She placed the newspaper in front of Yvonne. "This lady," she said, putting a finger on Marie Le Roi's name in the story about the bird flu.

Yvonne quickly read the story. "I'm not sure I understand," she said. "This Marie Le Roi owns a hat shop in Paris, but because of the bird flu, she can't get feathers, right?"

KC put the printout on top of the newspaper. "It's the same lady," she said. "She sent this e-mail!"

KC and Marshall took turns explaining

how they went into the craft shop, and how the owner gave KC the paper to draw on. "I think he stole the turkeys!" KC said.

Yvonne studied the newspaper story and the e-mail. "Oh my goodness!" she said. "These two are brother and sister. She calls him *mon frère,* which means *my brother.* And she signed it *votre soeur, your sister*!"

Yvonne looked at the paper again. "Her last name is Le Roi, and his is Leroy," she said. "I'll bet he changed the spelling of his name when he came to this country."

Marshall added, "He knew she needed feathers, so when he heard about all the turkeys on the National Mall, he figured out how to steal them."

"But how was he going to get the feathers to his sister?" KC asked.

"I don't know," Yvonne said. "But she says she will e-mail him again on Friday. That's tomorrow."

"So let's get the police to arrest the guy in the craft store!" KC said. "Then he'll have to give the turkeys back!"

"But we can't prove he took them, KC," Marshall said. "All he has to do is deny it."

Yvonne stood up. "We have to tell the vice president what you kids have dug up!"

Before long, the vice president knew the whole story. "This craft-store fellow is pretty bold, stealing all those turkeys," she said. "But he and his sister stand to make a lot of money. Because of the flu, bird feathers are in demand."

Mary Kincaid hit some keys on her laptop and brought up Google. She hit a few more keys. "Goodness," she said. "Some people in the hat business are willing to pay ten dollars for one perfect white turkey feather, and even more for some darker ones."

KC tried to do the math in her head. How many perfect feathers did Cloud have?

How many perfect feathers on 117 turkeys?

"Meanwhile, the turkeys are still missing," Yvonne said.

"Yes," the vice president said. "If you own a small craft shop, where do you hide nearly ten dozen turkeys?"

"Marsh and I think they must have used a truck," KC said. "I saw one parked at the National Mall yesterday. I thought you had it sent there, Ms. Kincaid."

The vice president looked at KC with wide eyes. "Goodness, I totally forgot!" she said. "Getting a truck to take the turkeys to Mount Vernon was on my list. It completely slipped my mind!"

"So maybe the truck KC saw was there for stealing the turkeys!" Marshall said.

"You could be right," the vice president said. "But where is it now?"

"I have a toy truck with remote control," Marshall said. "When I push a button, the truck comes back to me. Wouldn't it be cool if we could just push something and get the truck with the turkeys to come to us?"

Something clicked in KC's brain. She picked up the e-mail. "What if we e-mailed him back?" she asked.

"I don't get it," Marsh said. "E-mail the craft guy?"

KC nodded. "We could set up an e-mail account that's almost the same as his sister's. The e-mail would tell Mr. Leroy to sell the turkeys," she said. "Only he'd sell them to us. I mean to an FBI guy. After getting the turkeys, the FBI guy would arrest him!"

Everyone stared at KC.

"The e-mail would be from us, but Mr. Leroy would think it was from his sister," KC went on. She could feel butterfly wings flapping in her stomach.

"It would be an awesome trick!" Marshall crowed.

Yvonne plucked the printout out of KC's fingers. "We have her name and e-mail address and her brother's e-mail address right here," she said. She looked at the vice president. "Could it work?"

"Let's back up a minute," Mary Kincaid said. She took the e-mail from Yvonne. "It says here that Ms. Le Roi would e-mail her brother on Friday. That's tomorrow. Won't he think it's strange if she e-mails him today, a day early?"

KC had already thought about that. "Maybe the message we send could say she's in a hurry to get the feathers," she said.

"But what if she e-mails him tomorrow like she said she would?" Marshall asked.

"By then it will be too late," KC said, grinning. "We'll already have the turkeys, and he'll be in jail!"

"So if we're going to pull this off," the vice president said, "we have to do it today!"

8
Operation Turkey

In his office, President Thornton listened, then spoke to KC and Marshall and the vice president. "I like it," he said. "I hope Cloud appreciates what you kids are doing for him. He's one lucky turkey!"

The vice president looked at her watch. "It's nearly four o'clock here, so it's ten at night in France," she said. "I hope Leroy's sister goes to bed early. We don't want her calling him tonight!"

The president read the e-mail again that Yvonne and the vice president had written.

Bonjour, mon frère. Change of plans. Too difficult to send birds here. I have a buyer in USA. His name is Arnold. He will come to your shop at ten o'clock tonight. He will give you $50,000 in exchange for the live turkeys. Arnold will send me 1,000 feathers and sell the rest. Urgent: do not call or e-mail me. Make the exchange and I will call you tomorrow morning. *A bientôt. Votre soeur,* MLR.

The First Lady walked into the room. "Mr. Smiley is here," she said, and the FBI director followed her into the president's office. He was carrying a metal briefcase.

The president and Mr. Smiley shook hands. "Who do I give this to?" asked Mr. Smiley. "Fifty thousand dollars makes me nervous, even if it is fake money." He used a key to unlock the case, and it popped open. The president's desk lamp shone down on packs of hundred-dollar bills.

Marshall let out a gasp, and everyone laughed.

The president grinned. "Where did you get the counterfeit money?" he asked.

"That's a secret," Mr. Smiley said. He put a finger to his lips.

KC stared at the green bills. She had never felt so nervous. Her hands and fingers were cold, as if she'd been outside building a snowman.

"And we want it all back," Mr. Smiley went on, "after you've caught your turkey thief."

"What happens if Arnold gets to Mr. Leroy's shop at ten and Mr. Leroy isn't there?" KC's mom asked.

"Then it's over," the president said. "That means he didn't believe our e-mail, or he got tipped off somehow. We'll never see him or the turkeys again."

"Is Arnold ready?" the vice president asked.

The president nodded. "Ready and

excited," he said. "His brother, Dez, will be with him, and two FBI agents will follow as backup."

Mr. Smiley closed the briefcase and handed the key to the president. "Keep me in the loop," he said. "And now I'm going home to eat Thanksgiving dinner."

They watched the FBI director leave the room.

"It's almost time for our dinner, too," KC's mom said. "Your parents will be here soon, Marshall. You kids want to wash up first?"

"What're we having?" Marshall asked.

KC's mom winked. "That's a secret," she said.

Ten people sat around the president's dining room table—Marshall and his parents, Arnold and his brother, Yvonne, the vice president, KC and her mom, and the president. Everyone had the jitters because the shiny metal briefcase holding the fake money lay on a table in the corner.

KC's mom and Yvonne carried trays into the dining room. "Yvonne and I decided to serve our favorite foods," the First Lady said.

She and Yvonne set down steaming bowls of tomato soup. Goldfish crackers floated on the soup.

"Yay!" cried Marshall.

Then Yvonne added a giant platter of spaghetti. Next came a huge green salad. The First Lady placed a tall chocolate cake on the table next to the briefcase.

"These are all my favorites, too!" said Marshall. "How did you know?"

Lois smiled. "I asked your parents," she said. "Everyone dig in!"

"First I want to propose a toast," the president said. He stood and picked up his glass of cranberry juice. "To Yvonne and the First Lady, who prepared this delicious food, thank you. To KC and Marshall and the vice

president for convincing so many people to pardon their turkeys. And to Arnold and Dez for agreeing to rescue Cloud and his feathered friends!"

Everyone joined the toast by clinking glasses.

After dinner, Marshall's parents went back to their apartment. Marshall had his toothbrush and pajamas. He was staying at the White House overnight.

"Don't forget to feed Spike!" Marshall told his parents as they left. "Tarantulas like Thanksgiving, too!"

Arnold and Dez left to prepare for the money and turkey exchange.

The president and vice president locked themselves in the office with the money.

KC and Marshall went upstairs to KC's room. Her mom had told them that if they wanted to stay up for the excitement later, they had to get some rest.

But when KC threw herself on her bed at eight-thirty, she didn't feel at all sleepy. "I wonder where Cloud and the turkeys are right now," she said, cuddling with her stuffed animals.

"I wonder if there's any more of that chocolate cake left," Marshall answered from where he was lying on KC's rug. He yawned and closed his eyes.

KC tossed Mr. Gorilla at him, and Marshall used him for a pillow.

9
KC's Big Plan

About an hour later, KC's bedroom door opened. "Turkey time, kids," the president whispered.

The kids grabbed their jackets and followed the president. A clock at the bottom of the stairs announced that it was almost ten. Except for Marshall's parents, the same people who had eaten dinner together were in the kitchen.

Yvonne was heating milk for hot chocolate, and eight mugs were lined up on the counter.

KC slipped into the pantry. When she came out to the kitchen again, there was a bulge under her jacket.

"You fellows know what to do?" the vice president asked Arnold and Dez.

Arnold nodded. "Yup. We go to the Crafty Guy shop on New Street," he said. "If Leroy is there, we get him to take us to the turkeys. When he does, we hand over the money." Arnold and his brother wore baggy jeans, dark sweaters, and ski caps. KC thought they looked like bank robbers.

The briefcase stood on the counter, next to the mugs. Yvonne poured steaming milk into each, and the smell of hot chocolate filled the room.

Everyone walked outside to Dez's truck, sipping from their mugs. KC stayed in the truck's shadow, where her mother wouldn't see her.

"You'll have two FBI agents following your truck," the president told Dez. "You can talk to each other through devices in your caps. The agents will arrest Mr. Leroy as soon as you say he's accepted the money."

"And where will you be, dear?" KC's

mom asked the president. "I know you won't want to stay in the White House when all the excitement is out there!"

The president shook his head. "I'll be here with you and the kids, waiting for the good news."

He looked at Arnold and Dez. "Thank you two for doing this," he said, glancing at his watch. "Ten minutes."

"I'm a little nervous, sir," Arnold said. "Can I use your bathroom?"

Everyone laughed and walked back inside with their empty mugs.

KC stopped Marshall and pulled him behind Dez's truck.

"What are you doing?" Marshall asked her. "Let's go inside. It's cold out here!"

"It won't be cold in the sleeping bags," KC said. She put a foot on the truck's rear bumper and started to climb.

"What are you doing?" Marshall yelped.

"I'm getting in the truck, Marsh," KC said, throwing a leg over the tailgate. "Don't you want to see the turkey crook get arrested?"

"But that's crazy!" Marshall said. "We can't go with them!"

"Why not?" KC asked. She was sitting on the straw, fitting her legs into the opening of one of the sleeping bags.

"Because your parents will kill us and my parents will send me to my room for a million years!" Marshall said. "With no food!"

"Don't be silly," KC said. "Nobody said we couldn't go with Arnold and Dez. Besides, we'll have them to protect us. Are you getting up here, or am I going all by myself?"

Marshall stared at KC. "Protect us from what?" he asked.

"Whatever," KC said. She reached a hand out and helped Marshall into the truck. "Get inside the sleeping bag before they come back again."

Marshall climbed into the bag. "Why are we doing this?" he asked. "Can't we just stay home and wait, like normal people would?"

"Because I want to see, that's why," KC said. "Besides, I'm not normal." She shoved something crinkly at Marshall's sleeping bag.

"What's that?" he asked.

"A bag of popcorn," KC said. "Leave some for the turkeys."

Just then Arnold and Dez hurried out the back door and climbed into the truck. Arnold was carrying the briefcase filled with fake money.

KC and Marshall pulled their heads inside the sleeping bags like two turtles.

The pickup-truck motor started, and Dez pulled around the White House and onto Pennsylvania Avenue. KC peeked out of her sleeping bag and saw the FBI car following. She didn't know what the FBI agents would do if they saw her, so she kept low.

KC felt the truck slow to turn a corner. Then it slowed more, and the motor stopped. "We must be at the craft store," KC whispered into Marshall's ear. "Keep your head down!"

"Don't worry!" Marshall said.

They both heard the pickup's doors open, then close. They heard footsteps leaving the truck, then, five minutes later, returning.

"We'll follow you to the park," KC heard Arnold say.

"When do I get to count the money?" Aidan Leroy asked. They were standing only a few feet from where KC and Marshall were hiding.

"As soon as we count the turkeys," Arnold answered.

Then the brothers climbed back into the truck and it moved forward again. KC was trying to picture Aidan Leroy's car being followed by Dez's pickup truck, which was

being followed by the black FBI car.

KC lay in the sleeping bag looking up at the dark sky. This was a lot more fun than staying home waiting to hear what happened!

Soon they were driving under trees. There were no more lights. Dez's pickup went from riding over smooth streets to bumping over hills and holes. KC's and Marshall's sleeping bags were tossed up and down in the straw.

The truck stopped.

The kids heard doors slam, then voices. They put their heads back inside the sleeping bags.

"The turkeys are in the barn," Aidan Leroy's voice said.

"Show us," Arnold said.

Then the voices moved away.

KC stuck her head out of the sleeping bag enough to see Arnold, Dez, and Aidan Leroy walking toward a barn. They seemed to be in a dark field surrounded by trees.

One of the men carried a flashlight. Its beam bounced along the rough ground, then shone on the barn door.

She saw Aidan Leroy unlock the barn door and pull it open, revealing the rear of a big green truck. A thick rope was wound around the truck's back door, holding it closed. Aidan Leroy unwound the rope, then yanked open the door. Suddenly the night erupted with the sounds of 117 excited turkeys. A dim light inside the truck showed feathered bodies moving around. KC hoped Cloud was one of them.

The three men talked for a minute, but KC couldn't hear what they were saying. Then Aidan Leroy closed the truck door, and Arnold and Dez followed him around the truck, farther into the barn.

"Come on, Marsh," KC whispered. "Now's our chance!"

Marshall's head popped up. Pieces of

straw were stuck in his hair. "Chance to do what?" he asked.

"To see what they're doing," answered KC. "While they're inside the barn!"

"I'm having a nightmare," whimpered Marshall. "In a minute I'll wake up and be home safe in my own little bed."

KC slithered out of her sleeping bag. Keeping as low as she could, she slipped out of the truck bed onto the ground. Hoping Marshall was right behind her, she crawled toward the green truck in the barn.

Suddenly the truck's rear lights went on, blinding KC. She dropped to the ground, unable to see a thing.

10
Turkeys to the Rescue

KC looked up to see if the truck was backing out of the barn. It was not. But she could tell that all of the truck's lights were on, even in the front. Scrambling on her hands and knees, she crawled to the back of the truck and hid underneath. The rope that held the door shut was hanging in front of her eyes.

"Move over!" Marshall said as he came tearing after her. They both lay on the ground beneath the truck. Over their heads, they could hear the turkeys moving around and gobbling.

"Where are Arnold and Dez?" Marshall whispered. "What's going on?"

"They're in front of the truck," KC whispered. "I'll be right back." She turned and wriggled the length of the truck until she was between the front tires. The engine rumbled over her head. Straight ahead, she could see three pairs of feet. Two pairs were wearing heavy boots. The third pair of feet wore shiny black loafers. She listened, then wriggled back to Marshall.

"He's using the headlights so he can see to count the money," she said.

"Then what happens?" Marshall said. "If anyone moves this truck, we get squished."

"No, we won't," KC said. "The truck is way too high. It'll go right over our heads. Any minute now, the FBI guys will run in and arrest Mr. Leroy and we'll get our turkeys back!"

"Good!" Marshall said, pulling the bag of popcorn from inside his jacket.

Before he could reach into the bag, they both heard a Beatles tune echoing inside the barn.

KC froze. Was someone in the truck, playing the radio? Then she realized that she was hearing a cell phone's ring tone.

"Hello?" someone said. KC heard some muttered words and watched the black loafers walk to the rear of the truck. Aidan Leroy's feet stopped ten inches from KC's nose.

"Hello?" he said again. "Yes, I can hear you now. I'm with Arnold. He brought the fifty thousand, just as you said. I was counting it when you called."

KC's heart nearly stopped. Leroy had to be talking to his sister in France! Now he would find out that this was all a trick to catch him!

"What?" he cried. "I don't believe . . . !"

Without even realizing what she was doing, KC wrapped the dangling rope around one of Leroy's feet. Three seconds later, he took off running. He fell, and the rope yanked open the truck's rear door. In

the light shining from inside the truck, KC could see Leroy trying to untangle the rope from his foot.

KC snatched the bag of popcorn from Marshall's hands, crawled from beneath the truck, and threw the popcorn at Leroy. Right away, dozens of hungry turkeys flew out of the truck and landed on top of the panicked crook.

Two FBI agents bolted out of the woods and jumped onto the pile of turkeys. There was so much noise and confusion that KC forgot to listen for Cloud's little silver bell.

The next day, the First Family and Marshall drove the turkeys to Mount Vernon. KC and Marshall stood with Lois and the president, watching the turkeys strut about in the meadow. KC watched Cloud until he disappeared among all the others.

"Now I can see why George Washington

loved living here," KC's mother said. Mount Vernon was beautiful under the warm November sun. George Washington's home was surrounded by farmland and woods and fields. Horses and cattle roamed the pastures, and chickens wandered about looking for things to eat.

"I want to live here," Marshall said. "I could feed the animals."

"Nice idea, Marshall," the president said. "You could volunteer to work here when you're in college."

"What will happen to Mr. Leroy?" KC asked.

"Jail," the president said.

"Speaking of jail," KC's mother said, "you two are still going to be grounded for sneaking out last night."

"But if we hadn't stopped him, Mr. Leroy would have gotten away!" KC said.

"Nonsense," her mother said. "We had a

marine and two FBI agents on the case. We didn't need two fourth graders!"

"It was so cool rounding up the turkeys!" Marshall pitched in. "They were running all over the woods!"

KC watched two turkeys chase each other across the meadow. "Anyway, I have an idea for next Thanksgiving," she told the president.

He put his hand on her shoulder. "I can't wait to hear it," he said.

"I can," muttered Marshall.

Everyone laughed.

"Tell us your idea, KC," her mother said.

"Well," KC said, "if we pardoned one hundred and seventeen turkeys from Congress this year, just think how many we could get next year if we asked all the governors and mayors!"

Did you know?

Did you know that turkeys have been presented to the President of the United States since the 1800s? This tradition dates all the way back to when Ulysses S. Grant was president! But early on, turkeys weren't always pardoned. In fact, many turkeys presented to the president were eaten!

No one knows for sure when the practice of turkey pardoning started, but some people believe it began with Abraham Lincoln. In one story, Lincoln's son Tad asked his father to write a presidential pardon for the turkey that was meant for the family's Christmas dinner. Lincoln granted his wish. Both John F. Kennedy and Richard Nixon also spared turkeys while president, but George H. W. Bush was the first to formally pardon a Thanksgiving turkey in 1989.